THE BARD

Highland Heroes
Book Five

by Maeve Greyson

ARE YOU SIGNED UP FOR DRAGONBLADE'S BLOG?

You'll get the latest news and information on exclusive giveaways, exclusive excerpts, coming releases, sales, free books, cover reveals and more.

Check out our complete list of authors, too!

No spam, no junk. That's a promise!

Sign Up Here

www.dragonbladepublishing.com

Dearest Reader;

Thank you for your support of a small press. At Dragonblade Publishing, we strive to bring you the highest quality Historical Romance from the some of the best authors in the business. Without your support, there is no 'us', so we sincerely hope you adore these stories and find some new favorite authors along the way.

Happy Reading!

CEO, Dragonblade Publishing

Additional Dragonblade books by Author Maeve Greyson

Highland Heroes Series

The Guardian

The Warrior

The Judge

The Dreamer

The Bard

The Ghost

CHAPTER ONE

Highlands of Scotland
Clan Greyloch's keep
Early March 1704

THREE DAYS INTO the visit, and he still hadn't been shot. Considering the intensity of Lady Sorcha's threat, Sutherland MacCoinnich considered his lack of injury nothing less than miraculous.

He shifted in the sumptuous depths of a leather armchair. "Quite the library, eh? Rivals *Tor Ruadh*'s even." The only space in the enormous room not covered with manuscripts was the entrance and an array of tall windows overlooking a dreary garden struggling to recover from winter.

Magnus de Gray, Sutherland's long-time friend and brother in arms, slowly nodded while drumming his fingers on the armrests of a matching chair. "That it is," he said as he looked around. The leather of his seat squeaked in protest as he leaned toward Sutherland and lowered his voice. "Ye've still not seen her or heard anything, yet?" He cast a glance at the door. "I havena been able to glean a single hint of her whereabouts from any of the servants. Never have I seen such loyalty." He shot another look at the entrance, then shook his head. "I dinna think she's even here. Has Greyloch still said nothing? The man has to know what happened between the two of ye."

"Not a bloody word about her gracing us with her presence nor last summer's damned bet, no matter how many hints I place in every conversation." Sutherland rose, angled his chair to better face the entry to the library, then sat back down. "And that is why I willna be exposing my back to any door until this feud between the lovely Lady Sorcha and myself is settled."

The chieftain of Clan Greyloch had been agreeable enough at the prospect of a meeting to discuss business between the two clans. The congenial man had even welcomed them as though no undercurrent of hostility existed. Still, the first three days at Castle Greyloch had been strange. The chief had seemed too busy for them at every turn, barely sparing a moment long enough for a few words even during oddly rushed meals. Sutherland had mixed feelings about this visit that his brother, Chieftain MacCoinnich, had insisted upon.

Of course, he had wondered if he would survive another encounter with Lady Sorcha. The thought of her triggered a wicked smile. He had to admit he looked forward to a fresh duel with the fiery lass. After all, she was one of very few women he had never been able to charm.

In all honesty, he truly regretted his badly handled visit the past summer. His careless wager had somehow reached the lady's ears and did not set well with her. It hadn't set well with him, either, when it ended up costing him a barrel of whisky. Lady Sorcha's promise to shoot him if he so much as rode past Castle Greyloch's gates again was disappointing, as well. He couldn't believe the woman had gotten so angry about his betting he would have her bedded on his first night at their keep. Could she not see it as a compliment to her loveliness?

A narrow section of bookshelves behind the massive mahogany desk in front of them shifted with a low, groaning creak like the opening of a tomb. It slowly swung open.

He took to his feet and stepped behind the broad back of his chair but stopped at drawing a weapon. Instinct bade him wait until he knew who approached, while at the same time, his mercenary readiness tensed him tighter than a bowstring.

Magnus remained seated, giving him a side-eyed look as though he thought him mad. "Ye look a fool, ye ken?"

Sutherland ignored him, keeping his focus locked on the slowly opening panel.

Chieftain Robert Greyloch sidled his hulking frame into the room, giving the bookcase a critical up and down scowl as he shoved it back in place. "Damn thing. Sticking again." His irritation disappeared as he turned and lumbered over to a chair large enough for three men. As he pulled it back from the desk, he gave an apologetic nod. "Forgive the delay in our sitting down to discuss business, gentlemen. It's calving time. A verra busy season for our clan to ensure the continued success and growth of our prized cattle." His apologetic look shifted to Magnus, then returned to Sutherland. "Since the MacCoinnichs are curators of the finest breed of horses in all of Scotland, I'm sure ye understand." He hooked his thumbs in the pockets of his waistcoat and chuckled at Sutherland. "Ye'd do better to face the chair this way, lad." He jerked a thumb toward the wall of books behind him. "When Sorcha returns from the village today, she'll enter the library the same way I did. But ye do well to take cover. I feel sure she's intent on keeping the oath she made the last time the two of ye met."

So Magnus had been correct. Lady Sorcha had been away all this time. But she returned today. Sutherland found himself looking forward to it more than fearing it. "I appreciate the warning, Chieftain." He returned the chair to its original position, thankful Greyloch's good humor appeared to be as massive as his size. While he matched the chief in both height and build, he had never seen a man with hands so large. The old warrior's fists were broad as shields.

Determined to ensure there was, in fact, no ill will between them, Sutherland held out his hand. "Since we are finally speaking openly about the matter, allow me to extend my apologies regarding my behavior last summer." He twitched a shoulder, feeling a bit like a lad confessing about something he knew he shouldn't have done. "I meant no harm or insult to the lovely Lady Sorcha, but I do regret behaving in such a roguish manner."

Greyloch rumbled out an even deeper chuckle as he grabbed hold of Sutherland's forearm and squeezed hard enough that he nearly crushed his bones. "I accept yer apology, sir, but dinna fash yerself." He winked, still holding tight to Sutherland. "My daughter can take care of herself quite well, and I understand yer position completely. There once was a time when I was known to throw down a wager or two when it came to a challenging conquest."

Directing Sutherland to sit, he took his own chair. A glint in his eye, he settled back, stroking his closely cropped beard. "But all jests aside, ye would do well to tread lightly around her when she arrives. I fear she possesses her mother's fire and tendency to foster a grudge— forever." All levity left him as his silvery head tipped forward. "God rest her soul," he added quietly.

"God rest her soul, indeed." Sutherland wasn't quite certain what to say next. When last they had visited, he'd realized the rumors about the great love Chieftain Greyloch and his wife had shared were not rumors but truth. The man still seemed as stricken with grief as he had last summer.

"It's been well over two years now since that damned accident robbed me of my lady love." Greyloch shifted, heaving out a deep sigh as he scrubbed a hand across his face. He sat taller and looked at each of them with a strained smile. "But we must try and move on, aye?"

Sutherland wished he could ease the man's lingering pain, but all he could do was provide a distraction. "Aye, Chief, and while Clan MacCoinnich's losses canna begin to compare with yer own, we're attempting to move on from our own sorrows as well."

"I heard of the Neal uprising." Greyloch leaned forward, resting his forearms on the desk. "Shameful ungratefulness after all the MacCo-innich did for that clan. Prospered it well beyond what old Neal would ever have done." The intensity of the man's stare tightened like an arrow about to be released. Chieftain Greyloch might be getting on in years, but nothing about the man appeared diminished in any way. "Why did the MacCoinnich release them so easily from their oath of fealty? And gave them half the lands along with a share of the herds to boot? The man actually gave them the glens to the south? Those fine glens abutting the Campbells?"

"Aye, sir. But it was a complicated matter, ye ken?" Sutherland wasn't about to lay out his brother Alexander's choices and the why's of them to the chieftain. The ending of the feud with the Neals had come at great cost, but the decisions made had been necessary. Not only for the good of the clan but for the protection of the MacCo-innichs politically. Sutherland gave Chieftain Greyloch a look he hoped the man would understand and not take offense. "Such a story is better left for yerself and the MacCoinnich to share over a dram or two."

"Speaking of which," Greyloch thumped both hands on the desk and pushed himself to his feet, "it appears I have forgotten my manners. I'm sure yer throats are dry, and yer bones are cold from this dreary day. 'Tis still bitter cold for this to be early March." He went to an amply stocked sideboard and filled three glasses. Waving them forward, he held one up. "Come, gentlemen. I refuse to risk spilling this fine whisky by toting it over to ye."

Sutherland and Magnus didn't have to be invited twice. Both joined Greyloch and gladly accepted their drinks. Sutherland relished the rich burn down his gullet, while the heady fumes filled his nose. Nothing warmed a man's soul nor relaxed his mind quite like a good whisky.

The creaking of the bookcase door behind him and the click of a pistol abruptly interrupted his appreciation of Greyloch's fine blend.

"Ye will do me the courtesy of turning, Master MacCoinnich. I prefer to look a man in the eyes when I shoot him."

Lady Sorcha's melodious voice was laced with more venom than an adder. Sutherland fought the urge to rub at the hairs standing on end across his nape. Instead, he downed the rest of his drink in one gulp and returned the glass to the sideboard. He had been warned more than once that his womanizing ways would be the death of him. He reckoned death by the hand of a beautiful lass was as good a way to go as any.

Slowly turning, he held out his arms. Might as well provide the lady with a broader target. He came close to stumbling as he faced her. May the heavens help him, the woman was still lovely as hell even with a pistol pointed at his chest. Tall and slender as a graceful willow, with long hair the color of a red deer's newly born fawn. Eyes a startling greenish-gold, honed in on the sighting of her prey. Lady Sorcha Greyloch possessed a fierce, untamed beauty. She was definitely more intoxicating than any drink.

"Would ye grant me one last request, dear lady?"

"Why should I?"

Fire and fury flashed from her. What passion this bonnie lass possessed. Damnation, he wished she didn't feel so ill toward him. What he wouldn't do for a chance to win her over. Perhaps he might accomplish it yet. After all, as long as he wasn't dead, there was hope.

With a contrite dip of his chin, he took a step forward, keeping his arms extended. "Aye, my dearest lady, ye speak the truth of it. Ye are in no way bound to grant me a last request, but still, I beg ye to search what I'm certain is yer generous nature and choose to hear me out, even though I am so undeserving."

"Come now, daughter," Chieftain Greyloch urged, utterly failing at hiding his amusement. "It wouldna be Christian to shoot the man without hearing him out." He moved to stand beside Sutherland. "Be a good lass, now, and let the man speak his piece, aye?"

Weapon steady and still leveled at her target, Lady Sorcha's eyes narrowed even more. Sutherland could tell she knew her father thought this all a jest. He prayed she wouldn't kill him just to prove the man wrong. After a few moments, she gave a regal nod. "Speak yer request then. But know this, just because I hear it doesna mean I shall grant it, ye ken?"

Just to buy himself a bit more time and maybe even a tad of the lass's favor, Sutherland dropped to one knee. Surely, the woman wouldn't shoot a man kneeling at her feet. "All I ask, m'lady, is that ye grant me yer forgiveness for behaving like an ill-mannered cur. Please, I beg ye find it in yer heart to understand why I couldna help myself. The temptation was just too great. Yer beauty addled me, so I lost all ability to reason."

The pistol didn't waver. Lady Sorcha's head tilted slightly as one of her delicate brows arched higher. "So, ye're saying the fault of yer uncomely behavior is mine?"

"Aye, m'lady." He was a dead man for sure. He could tell it by her tone. Since he was already condemned to die, maybe he should ask for a kiss as well. Might as well leave this world with the taste of a fine lass on his lips. "Dear woman, truly, I had never beheld such a rare loveliness as ye possess, and a man is always more motivated to win a fair lady's approval when a wager is involved. Ye ken it's our nature to compete—to strive for our lady love's hand. The bet drove me even harder to win a sweet kiss from yer divine lips."

"My divine lips?" she repeated. Her contempt appeared tempered with the amusement of a spider toying with its prey. "I'm the fairest woman ye've ever met, ye say? And ye needed the bet to give ye the courage to try and seduce me?"

"Absolutely, m'lady. 'Tis the honest truth. I swear it." Sutherland assumed the most woeful look he could manage. "I pray the angels are as lovely as yerself, m'lady. My death willna be so bad then, although, I'm certain, they willna be able to console me if ye dinna grant me yer forgiveness and maybe even a last kiss so I might find rest in the hereafter."

Lady Sorcha blew out a very unladylike snort. "If our stables were filled with as much shite as ye just spewed, our livestock would drown in it. I shouldha worn my boots. Ye've piled it arse-high in here."

"Daughter!" Chieftain Greyloch strode over and plucked the pistol out of her hand. "Such language! Enough of this foolishness now. Accept the man's apology and be done with it. At least he asked yer forgiveness, and might I also add, he didna spread unseemly rumors about ye like some wouldha done once ye spurned them."

"A man will apologize for anything when he's facing the barrel of a gun." Lady Sorcha lifted her chin and pinned a damning glare on Sutherland.

Even without the gun pointed at his chest, Sutherland remained on his knee. Timing was everything in battles such as these.

Magnus stepped forward. "I assure ye, m'lady, that is the most heartfelt apology from this man that I have ever witnessed."

Sutherland kept his gaze locked on the lady, but the sound of liquid being poured told him Magnus had stepped forward to pour himself another drink—not swear to Sutherland's character. Magnus then appeared at his side, whisky in hand.

"And gun or not, I swear Sutherland is far too short-sighted *and* too stubborn to say anything he doesna mean—well, for the most part." Magnus lifted his glass in a toast, then downed it. "The man is honest to a fault. Most times. I swear it."

"Ye are not helping," Sutherland said, ready to knock Magnus on his arse. Raising his voice, he turned his attention back to Lady Sorcha, determined to win at least an amicable look from the lass and maybe even the hint of a smile. "All flowery words aside, m'lady, I am sorry for the bet. It was childish, pompous, and a poor choice indeed. My mam wouldha cuffed me hard were she still walking this earth. I do beg yer forgiveness—whether ye're still intent on killing me or not."

The lady rolled her eyes, gave the men a wide berth, and poured herself a glass of wine. "Why did Chieftain MacCoinnich send the two of ye rather than come here himself? Does he think so little of Clan Greyloch? It might be true we're a small clan, but it's apparent we have something he not only wants but needs. Would that not warrant a visit from the chieftain himself rather than a meeting with two of his lessers?"

"Sorcha Elaine! Where in heaven's name are yer manners?" Greyloch pointed toward a sitting area in front of the windows. "Let us all sit and get to the meat of this matter. That is, if my sharp-tongued daughter hasna already dissuaded ye with her insults."

Dissuaded? Nay. Intrigued? Aye, and for certain. Lady Sorcha possessed the sort of fire Sutherland admired. She always had. And if there was anything he loved more than the lasses, it was a challenge. He rose from his knee, poured himself another drink, and joined them. Raising his glass, he hid a smile as Chieftain Greyloch and Magnus seated themselves in the only pair of chairs available, leaving a small, two-person sofa as the only remaining place to sit.

"Da!" Lady Sorcha glared at her father.

Greyloch gave her a sharp look, then jerked a nod at the sofa. "Nay, daughter. Ye will sit beside the man and behave yerself. 'Tis yer penance for yer unladylike language and forgetting yer manners after Master MacCoinnich did his part by offering a heartfelt apology."

"Heartfelt apology, my—"

"Sorcha!" Greyloch's tone rang with parental warning.

"I shall be happy to stand," Sutherland offered with a gallant bow. "Please, m'lady. Have the sofa all to yerself with my blessing."

The lady bristled even more. She stomped over to the couch, dropped down with a huff, then smacked the cushion beside her. "By all means, Master MacCoinnich, please do sit beside me. I promise not to bite."

Bite away, lass. He wouldn't mind a nibble or two from this fair darling. His man parts took even more notice of the situation, forcing him to adjust the folds of his kilt to hide the bulging in his trews. He settled down beside her, pleased to discover that the cozy piece of furniture tucked them together quite nicely. In fact, if he dared shift the barest bit to his right, his shoulder and flank might actually brush against her. He resettled himself in the seat, taking care to rest a forearm across his lap to cover the evidence of his interest. He cleared his throat. "Now, as to yer question about Chieftain MacCoinnich assigning this visit to myself and Master de Gray?"

"Aye?" Lady Sorcha encouraged with a defiant glare.

"Rest assured that Chieftain MacCoinnich holds Clan Greyloch in the verra highest esteem." He paused, glancing over at Chief Greyloch to ensure the man knew he wasn't just dancing about and flattering with words to make peace with the man's daughter. "The size of a clan doesna guarantee its greatness. It is a clan's courage and honor that matters." He looked back at Lady Sorcha and smiled. "It hasna been so many years since Clan MacCoinnich's ranks were decimated to less than a dozen. But we didna give up after the morbid sore throat tried to kill us all. We pushed onward and fought hard to get where we are today. Even survived the massacre at Glencoe. We sense that same courage and honor in Clan Greyloch, and we are proud to call ye allies."

"Be that as it may..." Lady Sorcha gave a graceful nod paired with a sly smile. "Ye didna answer my question. Why are ye here rather than yer chieftain?"

Sutherland held his breath to keep from laughing aloud. Bless his soul, she was a stubborn minx, and he loved it. "I know horses and their needs far better than my brother. Alexander shines when it comes to planning battles, but when it comes to the precious breed that all of Scotland craves, Alexander only knows which end eats and which end shites."

By all that was holy, had the lady actually almost smiled? Not wishing to lose any progress he might've made with the enchanting mistress of Castle Greyloch, Sutherland turned his attention back to her father. "That is why I am here rather than Alexander. Our stable master and I are in agreement. The glens remaining within Clan MacCoinnich's borders are not large enough for our stock. Without more grazing choices, we'll not be able to increase the herds as we had planned. Grazing rights on Clan Greyloch's lands would help us continue the growth we had hoped to achieve over the next few years."

Greyloch didn't respond. Instead, the intensity of his glare sharpened as he locked eyes with his daughter.

Lady Sorcha gave the slightest shake of her head.

"Ye wish us to turn over our lands to the MacCoinnich herds?" the chief clarified. "When ye ken as well as I that yer herders will accompany yer horses and could verra well interfere with the effective grazing of our own prized Highland cattle? Is this yer poor attempt to expand yer borders and swallow up Clan Greyloch like ye did Clan Neal?"

This time it was Magnus's turn to give a warning shake of his head in Sutherland's direction. The silent signal advised that words needed to be chosen with care and not allow tempers to speak. Sutherland dipped his chin in acknowledgment that the message had been received, but Magnus's warning was unnecessary. Chieftain Greyloch's inquiry was valid. Sutherland expected no less from the man.

"We would never attempt such, sir. Our solicitor would draw up a document stating our full intent for the benefit of both clans that would also offer Clan Greyloch a percentage in the profits from the sale of any herds rotated through yer lands." That should ease some of their doubts. MacCoinnich horses brought a dear price, and buyers traveled from far and wide to purchase the much sought after breed.

"What percentage?" Lady Sorcha asked.

He had wondered how long she'd be able to remain quiet. She had fidgeted beside him like a worm in hot coals. Lady Sorcha was not a woman content to sit quietly and keep her thoughts to herself. Curious, he decided to see just how much she would say instead of allowing her father to negotiate the agreement. Just a wee test to see if this lass was as clever as she was beautiful.

Rumors hinted that it was she who truly ran the clan. The whispers had also claimed her father was too addled with age to handle the duties of a chieftain. Sutherland barely controlled his amusement at that idiocy. Chieftain Greyloch was definitely in full possession of his faculties. Rumors of his weaknesses were false and probably a sham propagated by the chief himself out of craftiness. So, what of the rumor about Lady Sorcha's assistance with controlling the clan?

"Twenty percent," Sutherland said in a tone that dared her to argue. Alexander had given him permission to go as high as fifty, but they didn't have to know that—at least, not yet.

She gave him a look that said he could go straight to hell. "Preposterous! Ye mean to have yer horses clip our pastures clean and only offer us twenty percent? Nay, I say! Keep yer beasts on yer own land or risk getting shot."

He warmed even more to the game, daring to shift so close the delicious heat of her caressed his thigh. "I am quite open to negotiation, m'lady. What do ye propose?"

Her gaze dipped to the lack of space between them, but she held her ground—even dared to scoot closer, so the length of her fine long leg pressed firmly against his. *Damnation.* The woman was trying to kill him. He resettled his arms across his lap to conceal his admiration that was growing stiffer by the minute.

"Sixty-five percent," she said, pausing for a sip of her wine. Lowering her glass, she graced him with a calculating smile. "Whilst horses and cattle graze in different ways, the herds will have to be managed carefully to prevent stripping the land bare and rendering it useless for either of them. Not only will we be sharing our land, but it will also take more of our herders to ensure the animals are moved properly from glen to glen without issue."

"Forty percent." Maybe if he made her negotiate longer, she would move closer still—Lord Almighty, what he wouldn't give to get her into his lap.

She didn't blink those gorgeous eyes of hers that had shifted to a piercing golden shade rather than the earlier hazel green. "Seventy percent."

"Daughter!"

Chieftain Greyloch barked out the word, but Lady Sorcha held up a finger to silence him without breaking her gaze from Sutherland's. "What say ye Master MacCoinnich?"

"I say ye're going the wrong way, m'lady." Emboldened by her daring, he took her hand and lifted it for a kiss. "Fifty percent and the finest colt born to the herd this spring belongs to ye personally. I shall see to its training myself so ye'll have a fine new mount to ride when it comes of age." He allowed his lips to linger on the silkiness of her skin a bit longer to help her decide.

"Fifty percent and my pick of the foals born to the herd every year ye make use of our lands. Be it a colt or not that I choose, one foal comes to Greyloch stables each year. What say ye?" With a smug look, she pulled her hand free of his.

"Fifty percent, yer pick of the foals every year, and a kiss to seal the bargain." He couldn't resist. Her full lips looked as delectable and succulent as fresh berries. Damn, he was starving for a wee taste.

"Done, sir." She brushed a glancing kiss across his cheek as she rose and hurried to take a stance beside her father's chair. "A fair and suitable agreement. Do ye not agree, Da?"

Chieftain Greyloch beamed with a self-satisfied grin. "Well done, daughter. Shall we drink on it, sirs? Then I shall have our own solicitor draft the document for yer clan solicitor's perusal, aye?"

"Not yet," Sutherland said as he slowly stood. The woman might think herself clever with that harmless peck on his cheek, but he wasn't about to let her off that easily. "Our bargain isna sealed as yet, m'lady. There is still the matter of the kiss."

"Ye received yer kiss, sir. On yer cheek." Victory sparkled in her eyes. The lass was so pleased with herself, she could barely stand still.

"Nay, m'lady. That wee pecking was little more than a greeting to a friend or a brother." He took a step closer. "I am neither. I am a man looking to seal an agreement once papers are drawn and signatures are rendered." He moved forward again until he stood close enough to take her in his arms. "Or are ye afraid?" he asked softly.

"Afraid?" She spit out the word like throwing down a gauntlet.

Sutherland resettled his stance. Aye, he'd read the vixen correctly. The lady wouldn't tolerate anyone thinking her fearful of anything. "Aye, m'lady. Afraid. We're hardly unchaperoned. Yer father sits right here. What else could it be holding back yer gift of a proper kiss other than fear of me?"

"My own good sense and ensuring ye realize ye've not been forgiven for being such an arse!" She didn't retreat, but nor did she step forward.

Chieftain Greyloch sidled around in his chair to improve his view, his grin stretching into a full-blown smile.

Sutherland held out a hand as though asking the lady to dance. "A *genuine* kiss to bind our bargain is just that, and I assure ye, m'lady, I know damn good and well ye've not forgiven me." It took every ounce of control he possessed to keep from pulling her into his arms and crushing her against him. A groan almost escaped him at the sight of her wetting her lips. He refused to retreat. She would learn he was as stubborn as she.

It was when her eyes narrowed the slightest bit, and her jaw tightened that Sutherland knew he had won.

Lady Sorcha closed the space between them, wrapped her arms around his neck, and pressed her curves against his hardness with daring tightness. Her lips brushed across his as she spoke, "Well? Get on with it then."

He tangled his fingers in the braid at the base of her neck, tilted her back, and wrapped his other arm around her waist. With her locked closer, he took her mouth, pouring every ounce of frustration, desire, and admiration she had stirred within him into the kiss. She tasted of wine and the firm realization that one kiss from this rare woman would never be enough.

Her embrace tightened, and she opened her mouth wider, returning his ferocity. She inflamed him more than any woman ever had before. Hell's fire, if she didn't kill him with a pistol, she would surely kill him with the sheer obsession to possess her. Before he could stop, he groaned and pressed his hardened length into her softness even more.

Lady Sorcha broke the kiss. Pushing herself out of his arms, she straightened her clothes as well as her hair. "There, sir. Is that kiss a good enough seal to our bargain until proper documentation is available?"

"Aye, m'lady," he managed to utter. "That kiss most definitely sealed everything."

CHAPTER TWO

I F SHE HAD possessed any doubts, Sutherland's kiss had vanquished them.

He was most definitely the one for her. A perfect choice as husband and father to her future children. But she had to manage this campaign wisely. Just because he lusted after her didn't mean he would go so far as to ask her to take his name. She had to tempt him beyond reason without weakening in her own resolve in the process. If she gave in too quickly, he'd slip away like a fish stealing bait.

Sorcha drew in a deep breath and eased it out. Remain calm, calculating, and steadfast. Quite the monumental task after that kiss. She pressed her lips tighter together. Saints have mercy on her soul, if he kissed like that, what other fiery magic might he possess? Obviously, the rumors about the man's talents with women were not exaggerated.

"Excuse me, m'lady. The seating at the chief's table this evening?"

Sorcha snapped out of the delicious daze she had struggled with ever since the more than satisfying encounter in the library. "Masters MacCoinnich and de Gray to Da's left," she instructed Mrs. Finnia Breckenridge, Castle Greyloch's housekeeper for as long as Sorcha could remember.

Mrs. Breckenridge wrinkled her long, narrow nose as though she smelled something foul. "And the other two?"

The other two. Lady Delyth Culane and her bullish son, Garthin Napier. They had been at the keep almost a month now, blaming the weather for keeping them at Castle Greyloch longer than planned. The weather had grown a sight more stable, but still, they hadn't left. Sorcha gave a curt nod. "Master Napier at one end of the table and Lady Culane at the other."

"As far from the chieftain and yerself as possible, aye?" murmured the astute housekeeper. "And shall we double the guard at yer father's chamber door this evening? I received word the lady is most determined."

"Aye, most definitely double the guard," Sorcha agreed as they continued their inspection of the hall in preparation for the evening's meal. "I, too, was told the woman attempted four visits to Da's rooms last night alone. Poor Godfrey. He said he's too old to be chasing off a bitch in heat. Replace him with younger guards. Maybe she'll chase after one of them to warm her bed and leave Da alone." Sorcha came to a halt. "On second thought, replace Godfrey with Raibie and Kiff. Neither of them will be tempted with the likes of that one." She glanced around the large room, wishing she could simply order the unwanted guests packed up and carted off. With a conspiratorial nod, she lowered her voice. "I have no doubt those tonics the woman drinks are meant to get her with a bairn. I believe she'd lay with anyone in the keep to be able to claim Da as the father."

"Hmm." The housekeeper's response spoke volumes. Mrs. Breckenridge was completely devoted to Chieftain Greyloch. "And yet Himself swears he never invited them here for a wee visit as they claimed he did?"

"Adamantly." Sorcha continued inspecting the room, checking the table holding all the candlesticks the servants had cleaned and refilled for the evening.

Those of silver were meant for the head table and gleamed without a single fingerprint. The heavier iron candelabras were destined for the narrow side tables along the walls. Those had been scrubbed free of old wax drippings and oiled until they shone a lustrous black. The dark chandeliers hanging from above had also been cleaned and fitted with fresh beeswax candles. "I asked Da three times if he invited that cow and her son to come and visit. He swears on Mama's tomb that he did not."

"Then I believe Himself," Mrs. Breckenridge said, loyalty ringing in her tone. "It was probably that old Raibert Pearsley. I dinna trust that man one whit. If there's a loose woman to be found, Raibert Pearsley will find her, and ye ken as well as I how little store he places on a woman leading the clan. He's been the most outspoken against any decisions ye've made."

Sorcha agreed with Mrs. Breckenridge's assessment completely. Raibert Pearsley was one of Clan Greyloch's advisors and a likely suspect in trying to saddle her father with another wife in a bid to get him a son and a more acceptable heir than Sorcha—"a mere daughter" in the man's own words. And the rest of the advisors, and Da, too, had spent far too many of their waking hours trying to marry Sorcha off to the highest bidder. Said they were doing it for the sake of the clan. She had lost count of how many offers she'd refused. Apparently, many in Clan Greyloch feared a woman's leadership.

"Make certain all the advisors except for War Chief MacIlroy are aware that they are not to sit at the head table." Sorcha eyed the layout of the room again, then pointed to one of the draftier corners. "Move a table for the advisors to that spot just below the window. With all their hot air, they'll be plenty warm enough, I'm sure."

"I shall see it done." The housekeeper halted as they came even with the hearth closest to the archway leading to the kitchens. "Look at that! Still filthy as can be. Excuse me, m'lady. Apparently, it's time I lit a fire under a few lazy slugabeds."

"Thank you, Mrs. Breckenridge." Sorcha had no doubt the housekeeper would have that hearth clean enough to eat a meal off of within an hour's time.

"Sorcie!"

Sorcha turned, responding to the name her closest friends had called her since the three of them were wee bairns. Jenny Pratt, an orphaned lass Mama had taken in, the sister of Sorcha's heart if not by blood, waved from the entry hall as she shrugged off her cloak and shook it out.

"The rain's trying to turn to sleet again," Jenny announced with a disgusted shiver. "Old Aderyn says we've got another big snow headed our way. Reckon she's right?" The dark-haired girl brushed at the moisture beading up on her wool skirts. The cold had turned her nose and cheeks a bright scarlet that perfectly highlighted the deep blue of her eyes. "Have ye seen Heckie? I've nay been able to find him anywhere. He promised to sit with me at the meal tonight, but now I canna find him. Have ye any idea where he might be hiding? Ye know how I worry after him. Especially of late. I fear he might be having one of his spells. I have looked all over—"

Sweet Jenny always prattled nonstop. The only way to communicate with the lass was to jump in and talk. "I havena seen Heckie, but ye ken as well as I that he's usually in the stables 'round this time helping Mungo." Sorcha circled her friend and attempted to catch hold of her long enough to swipe away the water droplets collected on her shawl. Jenny was always in motion, keeping her plentiful curves bouncing. The lass left a trail of enjoyable chaos everywhere she went.

"I tried the stable," Jenny said, yanking her sleeves straighter as she moved closer to the fire. "Reckon he hid from me? He had to hear me calling. I'll box his ears if I catch him doing such."

Heckie MacIlroy completed their close-knit trio. The only son of War Chief Hector MacIlroy, the boy had grown up in the keep alongside Sorcha and Jenny. The three had played and fought like siblings for as far back as any of them could remember.

"If he promised to sit with ye, I'm certain he will. He's gotten better about not pestering and breaking his word so much, hasn't he?" Sorcha straightened Janey's lopsided shawl across her shoulders.

"Maybe he's left off pestering yerself, but not so with me. I wouldna be far off the mark if I called him a boldfaced liar whenever he opens his mouth on most days." Jenny turned and backed closer to the fire. She frowned at the servants buzzing about the hall. "My bottom's cold as death, but I reckon I better not lift my skirts to warm it with so many about."

"Ye best not," Sorcha warned. "Someone would surely tell Da, and he's still not happy about ye being in the guardhouse 'til well past yer bedtime."

"We were playing tables, and I was winning." Janey's innocent grin turned wicked. "Lined my purse quite nicely, if I do say so myself. I've nearly enough saved for that bolt of silk I saw in the shop at Edinburgh."

"Well, Da's not forgotten about it, so ye best behave for a while if ye ever hope to be allowed to visit Edinburgh again." Sorcha immediately lost interest in shielding her friend from her father's wrath as Sutherland and Magnus strolled into the room. "And there he is," she murmured under breath.

Jenny followed Sorcha's line of sight. "My goodness. The man's even more handsome than he was last summer. How is it he's not pale from the winter? He looks all..." Jenny grinned and wiggled like an excited puppy. "He looks all dark and dangerous."

Sorcha agreed completely. "It must be the beard," she mused aloud, knowing good and well that Sutherland's close-cropped beard was the least of his *dark and dangerous* look. She pressed a hand to her heart, remembering how hard his broad chest had felt when he had embraced her. As tall as she was, he had cradled her completely as though she was a wee slip of a girl. Sutherland MacCoinnich was a full head and shoulders taller than anyone she had ever met. Well, anyone except for Da.

"He looks like a pirate. A mountain of a pirate. I think it's the way he walks," Jenny continued. "And wasn't his hair more golden last summer?"

"It probably goes darker in the winter." Sorcha watched Sutherland as he and Magnus meandered beneath the gallery on the other side of the room.

Jenny's observation about his stride held merit. The braw warrior moved with the strength and surety of a man who conquered whatever he wished. She could see the flex and ripple of his huge legs as they moved beneath his kilt. Her breath caught as she remembered his massive arms doing the same when he'd held her. "Let's move closer to the window. The fire grows too hot," she said as Sutherland looked her way and smiled.

Jenny giggled. "I dinna think it's the fire that's heating ye." She scurried along at Sorcha's side. Not nearly as tall and long-legged, poor Jenny always struggled to keep up.

Sorcha shortened her stride for her friend's sake. "And now ye understand some of the many reasons as to why I have chosen him to be my husband."

"He's coming this way," Jenny said without moving her lips.

"M'lady," Sutherland said in a way that made the words feel like a sensual caress.

The richness of his deep voice had affected her the same way last summer. She hadn't revealed her weakness to it then, and she wasn't about to show it now. "Master MacCoinnich." She gifted him with a cool nod.

"*Master MacCoinnich?*" Sutherland took her hand and kissed it, peeking up at her with a devilish gleam in his eyes. "Not *Master MacCoinnich*, m'lady. Not after the kiss we shared. I beg ye call me Sutherland so I might replay the sound of ye saying my name in my dreams."

"Take care, *Sutherland*," Sorcha warned. "Ye'll have me searching for my boots again to wade through such empty flattery."

He rumbled out a deep laugh, all the while maintaining a hold on her fingers. "As ye wish, m'lady." He kissed her hand again and released it with what appeared to be certain reluctance. "Let there be only genuine conversation between us, agreed?"

"Agreed," Sorcha said, clasping her hands together to savor the feel of his touch. Belatedly remembering her manners, she inclined her head toward her friend. "Ye remember Mistress Jenny?"

"Aye." Sutherland gave a polite nod, then motioned Magnus forward. "Ye met Magnus de Gray during our last visit to Castle Greyloch, did ye not?" he asked Jenny.

"Aye, I did." Jenny bounced a quick curtsy. "'Tis good to see ye both again. Will ye be staying long this visit?"

"That depends," Sutherland said with a look that sent more thrilling heat through Sorcha.

"On the weather?" Sorcha supplied, determined to appear polite but nothing more.

"Aye, dear ladies," Magnus interjected with a glance toward the window. He shot a pointed look at Sutherland, then turned back to Sorcha and Jenny. "The weather and the preparation of the documents by yer clan's solicitor."

"I shall be certain the solicitor knows their importance over any other matters at hand." She maintained a detached air. Sutherland needed to think she would like him out of the keep as quickly as possible.

"No hurry, m'lady," Sutherland assured her. He moved closer. "No hurry at all."

"Did ye get to see the chapel yet?" Jenny asked like a child excited to show off a new plaything. "It wasna quite finished when last ye were here."

"I, for one, would love to see the chapel." With a gallant nod,

Sutherland offered his arm to Sorcha. "M'lady?"

Jenny gave Sorcha a look she understood all too well. Jenny planned to lure Magnus away, then Sorcha and Sutherland would have the chapel all to themselves. What better place to plant the seeds for future matrimony?

Magnus held out his arm to Jenny. She accepted it with a giddy smile, then pulled him forward and took the lead.

"Did yer father not say he built the chapel in honor of yer mother?" Sutherland asked as they followed.

He remembered. Womanizer or not, the man had remembered what her father had told him a year ago about the elaborate structure he had ordered built around her mother's tomb. Sorcha nodded. "Aye. The cornerstones were placed just three days after she was laid to rest."

"I am sorry about yer mother's loss," he said in a tone she had never heard him use before. The man sounded genuine. All his flirtatious pomp had disappeared. Left in its place was the kindness of a concerned friend.

"Thank...ye." This newest tactic caught her off guard. She knew how to counter the empty words and fawning gestures of a rogue. But kindness and caring could be deadly to any counter moves she possessed in her arsenal.

"Forgive me if I've upset ye," he hurried to say. "Yer father still seems quite filled with grief as well."

"Their love was rare and strong," she said quietly. "Even now, he struggles without her at his side." She quickened their pace as they entered the long covered corridor leading to the massive chapel behind the keep itself.

Most clan chapels were modest, dwarfed in size compared to other structures in the collection of buildings usually found within a fortress's walls. Not Castle Greyloch's chapel. More a cathedral than a small structure for worship, its vaulted roof rivaled the height of the keep itself. It was a wonder the building had been completed in two years. The place stood as a true testament to just how much the clan loved their chieftain and his lady.

"Majestic," Sutherland said in a hushed tone once they stood inside the nave.

The place smelled of holiness, peace, and hope. The lingering fragrance of the incense the priest burned added to the reverent air. A quietness stood guard like a gathering of unseen angels. The waning sunlight of the early spring day struggled to filter through the stained glass windows, casting a rainbow of colors across the polished floor. The windows had cost the clan dearly, but they had borne it without complaint, proud of Greyloch Chapel and the last gift they had been able to give their beloved lady.

Sorcha led the way to the aisle. Maybe her nerves would settle if she introduced Sutherland to Mama. There was no crypt for the chapel. Her mother's resting place was to the right of the altar, set upon a raised platform built into the southern transept. Flickering candles constantly kept lit by chapel servants, lent a soft glow across the ornate sarcophagus and effigy of her dearest mother. The sculptor had done well. Mama's likeness was both calming and unsettling.

With a hard swallow, Sorcha struggled to maintain some semblance of composure. It had been well over two years since a stumble down the turret steps had stolen Mama from them, but every time she looked at the lifelike effigy in eternal sleep, the pain of the loss became raw once again. "The Lady Amelda Tiernan Greyloch," she whispered as a tear escaped and trailed down her cheek.

Sutherland took her hand, eased an arm around her, and gently pulled her close. "I see now where ye get yer beauty," he said quietly as he hugged her hand to his chest.

"Mama was the one who possessed true beauty. Inside and out." She didn't attempt to pull away, instead, she leaned into him, allowing herself the luxury of drawing from his strength. She had always found coming to the chapel difficult, but she endured it for Da's sake. The place gave him solace, but it stirred too many precious memories for Sorcha's comfort.

She lost track of how long they stood there, Sutherland holding her, his strong silence more soothing than words could ever be. It was as though they were the only two left in the world, standing on the precipice of eternity.

The main door of the church thudded, shattering the heavy stillness. Hurried footsteps scuffled toward them, growing ever louder.

"Lady Sorcha! It's time."

The hushed call rang with urgency, hitting Sorcha like a splash of cold water. Mungo Greyloch, stable master in charge of the clan's prize stock, was a calm man. If he sounded an alarm, it was true. She stepped aside, hastily putting an arm's length of space between herself and Sutherland as the agitated man rounded the last pew.

"Lady Sorcha, it's yer Peigi. It's her time. She's baying and bawling something fierce."

"That canna be. She greeted me as usual when I visited this morning. She seemed finer as could be." Sorcha grabbed up her skirts to hurry to the call, then belatedly turned back to Sutherland. "Forgive me. I must go."

"Who is Peigi?" In two strides, he caught up with her and Mungo.

"Peigi's her wee one," Mungo said, huffing and puffing as he struggled to keep up. Both age and girth plagued the man. His fondness for food and drink had made him resemble the fine Highland cattle he tended.

"When her mother refused her, I nursed sweet Peigi and raised her as my own," Sorcha explained as they left the church and rushed across the courtyard.

"Ye nursed her? The daughter of the chief tended a calf?" Sutherland's teasing tone hit her ill.

"I couldna verra well let her die, now could I?" Sorcha increased her pace toward the thatch-roofed building where the cows about to calve were kept. It was too early in the year, and the Highland weather too fickle to allow the precious expectant mothers to roam. Too many newborn calves could be lost that way. She pushed inside and hurried to the stall in the farthest corner. Her sweet friend, the largest Highland cow ever to grace Clan Greyloch's herds, stood with her great legs in a splayed stance, swaying back and forth with her shaggy head hanging low. The bovine split the air with a loud, rumbling moo.

"Sweet Peigi, I'm here, *fear beag,* dinna fear." She scooped up a handful of the special grain mix she prepared each day as a treat for her. "Here, my wee one. Have a nibble to ease ye."

"*Wee one?*" Sutherland echoed.

As she entered the stall, she paused long enough to shoot a warning glare back at the man. Thoughtless fool. This was no time for jesting. What if Peigi died? Apparently, the man needed a lesson in compassion. "Aye, she is my little one, born so weak and sickly, her mother didna want her. I spent many a night in this stall, cradling this fine girl in my lap. I wouldna let her die then, and I willna let her die now. If ye canna be kind to my sweet lass in her time of need, ye can haul yer arse out of here, ye ken?"

All jesting fell away from him, replaced with a genuinely contrite look and a bowed head. "Forgive me, lass. I meant no harm. It's just...I believe she's the biggest coo I have ever seen." He studied the animal. "I've helped with birthing foals. Shall I join ye? I swear I'll be gentle with yer good lass and help her all I can."

The cow bellowed a loud cry that sounded like an adamant refusal.

"Nay, not just yet. She doesna ken ye and isna in the mood for introductions at the moment." Sorcha smoothed her hands down the shaggy animal's swollen sides, cringing as the poor thing's muscles knotted, then relaxed beneath her palms. "Ye must be strong, little one. Fight through this, aye? Just like ye did when ye were a wee one." As she had hoped, the more she spoke to the agitated cow, the calmer the beast became. She combed her fingers through the long ruddy strands of the hairy coat, then smiled up at him. "Is she not a bonnie lass? I've often wished my muddy brown locks were colored as pretty as hers."

With his powerful arms propped atop the stall gate, Sutherland nodded. "She is verra bonnie—as is her adopted mother, whose shimmering tresses are colored as rich and beautiful as a well-aged whisky." He locked eyes with her. "And I'm not just trying to charm ye, Sorcha, nor fill this fine stable with shite."

Her cheeks warmed. The man hadn't meant any harm with his jest, and she shouldn't have been so snappish. She forgave him with a smile. "I'm glad to hear it because the lads have quite enough shite to shovel."

All conversation was forgotten as the massive beast lurched to the side and pinned her to the wall. Squeezed between the rough boards at her back and the heavy cow at her front, she struggled to breathe. Bursts of light flashed across her field of vision as the bovine leaned harder against her and bayed with a mournful bellow.

"This way with ye now, my wee beastie, before ye crush yer mistress." Somehow, Sutherland convinced the shaggy animal to shift the other way. The beast went to its knees, then rolled to its side in the clean hay. He caught Sorcha up against his chest before she crumpled to the floor. "Are ye hurt? Can ye breathe, lass?"

The urgency in his voice warmed through her, as did the concern making his eyes seem all the bluer. She clung to him as she wheezed in slow, deep breaths. "Dinna fash, I'm fine," she said. But the more she recovered, the more she realized she wasn't fine at all. Sutherland's embrace threatened to disturb her breathing even more than the tremendous weight of the cow crushing her. "Thank ye," she whispered.

He didn't answer, just stared down at her, unblinking.

Every sense she possessed sharpened, demanding she pay heed and savor this man holding her as though he cherished her. The hard length of him against her triggered a deliciously dangerous aching. His heat. The beat of his heart. Everything about him made the aching worse.

With a gentleness that made her long to toss all caution and plotting aside, the beguiling man nibbled a hesitant kiss across her mouth, paused the span of a heartbeat, then increased the bond, gently opening her mouth with his.

The laboring cow rattled the stall with a loud bawling.

Sutherland quickly stepped aside but kept a tight hold of Sorcha's hand. Before she could kneel at the cow's side, he stopped her. "Things are different when I'm with ye, m'lady—*my* Sorcha." He spared a glance over at the animal and smiled. "But all that must wait for now since new life demands our attention."

"That it d-does." Heaven help her, she hadn't stammered since she was a bairn. She slipped her hand out of his and knelt beside Peigi, leaning over to place her mouth close to the cow's fuzzy ear. "Thank ye," she whispered and meant it. If not for the interruption, who knows what she might've done. Her determination and planning haunted her. If she weakened and gave over so easily to the man, he'd slip away as soon as he achieved his conquest. It was far too early in this game to fall helplessly into his arms.

"I see a wee pair of hooves and a nose. All is looking good. Instincts are guiding her now." Sutherland stepped back from the cow. "She looks to be doing well. We should step out of the stall and give her the room she needs."

"I'm staying right here." Sorcha angled around, sitting in the straw beside the animal's head.

Sides heaving, the cow strained, then struggled and returned to a standing position again.

"She canna find the placement she wants." He stepped out of the stall but kept the gate open, blocking the exit with his body. He waved her forward. "Come, lass. Give her space. I know she's docile enough, but she could accidentally crush ye. She's already come close to doing so once."

Sorcha stood but wasn't about to leave the stall. Not only did her pet need her comforting, she wasn't about to give Sutherland the idea that she would do his bidding whenever he asked. "I'm staying in here with her. All will be fine. She needs me close." Inwardly, she smiled at the loud snort her announcement drew until he wrapped his arms around her, picked her up, then set her feet back to the ground, right in front of him at the gate.

"Then ye will stand here where I can grab ye up and keep ye safe if need be, ye stubborn woman."

Momentarily speechless, she clenched her hands to her sides. How dare he do such a thing! She was not a child to be scolded and moved by force. But a little voice inside bade her admit that his act had secretly thrilled her. She scolded the idiotic wee voice in her head and gritted her teeth so hard her jaws ached. *Nay.* This was not acceptable, and he needed to learn that.

Peigi chose that moment to settle back down in the hay and, with a huge shudder, expelled her calf.

Sorcha held her breath, praying the mother would accept the baby. Relief and joy filled her as the animal nosed her offspring a few times, then busied herself with the task of cleaning the little one up.

"Well done, my wee one," she praised quietly. "Such a good mama ye are." She eased back a step and bumped into Sutherland, then turned and glared up at him. Time for his lesson in manners. "Ye will do me the courtesy of getting out of my way, Master MacCoinnich."

"*Master MacCoinnich?*" He didn't move, just widened his stance, and folded his arms across his wonderfully broad chest.

"Aye." She lifted her chin. If it was a battle he wanted, it was a battle he would get. "Move, *Master MacCoinnich.* Now."

He frowned and gave a slow shake of his head. "I willna be moving until ye address me properly."

"Ye will move," she said with a hard but useless shove against him. "And I did address ye properly, sir. At least I didna call ye an overbearing arse."

"Nay, woman." Sutherland leaned down until his nose was within a hair's breadth of hers. His stubborn heat embraced her, held her prisoner. "Whether ye wish it or not, the two of us are now on a much more familiar basis than *Master MacCoinnich*."

"In whose opinion?" Every time the man opened his mouth, he only riled her more. She wished to become his wife, not his property, nor someone expected to follow his every order. He would not tell her how to speak.

"This visit has taught me much about ye, m'lady," he said in a low, deadly tone. "And I've a feeling we're just getting started."

"Ye'll be taking yer hands off the Lady Sorcha," warned a voice Sorcha had known all her life. "Release the lady now or discover the true sharpness of my blade as it slides through ye."

Chapter Three

The bite of a sword between his shoulder blades brought his battle-hardened instincts to life. Sutherland spun and slammed his fist into the assailant's jaw. As the man flew backward, he spared him half a glance, ensuring the fool didn't move once he hit the ground. The intruder landed flat of his back several lengths down the stable's center aisle.

What an idiot to threaten him in such a way. Sutherland turned back to Sorcha, but she shoved around him before he could speak.

"Heckie!" she crooned as she knelt beside the unconscious man. A worried scowl puckered her brow as she framed his already swelling face between her hands. She shot a furious look back at Sutherland. "Did ye have to hit him so hard? Ye're three times his size."

More like four. But he didn't wish to sound vain. "I've never treated a sword at my back lightly, and I willna start now."

She had called the man *Heckie*. He looked like a *Heckie*. Tall, gangly, and a good wind would blow him away. Sutherland came to a halt at the lad's feet and stared down at him. "If he's willing to attack a man, he best be prepared for the consequences."

She glared up at him. "He's like a brother and was only trying to protect me. He didna ken if ye were making unwanted advances or not. Ye didna have to be such a brute about it."

Unreasonable scolding aside, Sorcha's fussing made him appreciate her fiery beauty even more. Her irritation colored her fair cheeks a lovely pink, and her eyes flashed with rage. The woman fascinated him. To be honest, she triggered something inside him, something no other woman had ever set off in him before. What was it about this fearless lass that drove him to possess her? And not just her body. Nay—much more. He found himself thinking of her as his own. His. No one else's. Ever.

"I repeat," he said as he fixed her with a reproachful look that he hoped would infuriate her even more. Sparring with the lass was delightful. "If ye stick a man with a sword, ye'd best be ready to handle the reaction, ye ken?"

"Well, ye dinna have to be such an arse about it," she snapped.

"Aye, m'dear one, I do." He gave her a condescending nod. "Ye'll find I can be the most relentless of arses when it comes to protecting myself and whatever I decide is mine." Then he strode out of the stable. He'd leave her to stew about that for a while, wondering if she would realize the depths of what he had just said. The more the woman used her wiles to toy with him, the more he enjoyed this game. Both his heart and gut lurched as he realized Lady Sorcha was not a woman to be loved then left behind. Nay, she was a dangerous creature who would take hold of a man, body and soul, and never let him go. He pulled in a deep breath and blew it out. So, where did that leave him? And what did he intend to do about her?

"Sutherland!"

Magnus emerged from the tents stretched over the roasting pits of the keep's outer kitchen. He jerked a thumb back at the spirals of smoke filtering up from the opened flaps of the makeshift shelters. "Salmon and boar. Clan Greyloch's hunting and fishing shall grant us a fine feast tonight." He cast a glance upward, looking wishful. "If Merlin were here, he'd be more than happy. Salmon is his favorite. Especially from the River Spey." Merlin, Magnus's falcon and devoted friend, had been left behind at Clan MacCoinnich's keep due to the uncertainties of the early spring weather.

"Ye know as well as I that yer wee buzzard is better off warm and safe at the keep. The children promised to keep him entertained." Sutherland looked past Magnus. "Ye left Mistress Jenny's company so soon?"

Magnus twitched with a sheepish flinch. "Mistress Jenny is a fine lass, but her love of conversation makes my head hurt. I had forgotten how much that woman chatters about absolutely nothing." One who usually kept to himself, Magnus preferred quiet.

Sutherland laughed. "I wouldha thought ye better equipped to handle such noise after a winter at *Tor Ruadh* around all the bairns." With Alexander's five children, Graham's two, and Ian's four, the keep was anything but peaceful.

"Who is that with Lady Sorcha?" Magnus frowned at something beyond Sutherland's right shoulder.

With a fair idea of who it was, Sutherland cast a glance behind him. The man in question limped along beside Sorcha, one hand holding his jaw while he draped an arm around her shoulders for support. "That is *Heckie*. Lady Sorcha's champion, who is much like a brother to her and foolhardy enough to threaten me with a sword jabbed in my back." Head tilted, he studied the man's impaired gait. "Apparently, he landed badly when I knocked him on his arse. She isna verra happy with me."

"The man's lucky to be alive," Magnus observed.

Sorcha shot him a stinging look as the two turned and disappeared into the kitchens.

"The man's luck willna hold," Sutherland mused. "Especially if he's permanently knocked me from Lady Sorcha's favor."

"Which reminds me," Magnus said as he turned his attention back to Sutherland. "Ye behave differently around her. Have we finally found the woman able to conquer the unconquerable Sutherland

MacCoinnich's heart?"

His friend's insinuation grated on his nerves. He waved it away like clearing smoke. "Ye ken as well as I how much I admire a strong woman. Lady Sorcha isna the sort a man flirts with to get his way." He wasn't about to discuss his fears regarding Sorcha's effect on him.

"Ye dinna admire strong women. Ye fear them," Magnus retorted. "I've seen ye go out of yer way to avoid yer brothers' wives."

"I respect them. I dinna fear them." The sky rescued him from further conversation by opening up the clouds and spilling out an even icier rain than earlier. "Time to find a fire and a drink," he announced as he ducked inside the nearest door.

Magnus hurried after him. "Lead the way, man!"

As they turned the corner and strode into the corridor, Sutherland collided with something soft and smelling of very strong perfume.

"Merciful heavens! The chieftain shall hear of yer carelessness, I grant ye that!"

"Forgive me, m'lady. Allow me to assist ye." He attempted to help the woman back on her feet but couldn't get a proper hand hold because of all her floundering and the abundance of ruffles, skirts, and wraps in the dim lighting of the passage. Heaven help him if he happened to latch on to something he shouldn't. "M'lady, stop struggling so I might help ye stand."

The irritating creature continued her flopping like a fish out of water. "Nay, sir! Unhand me, I say!"

"Magnus, help me with this woman." He failed to understand why the infernal creature couldn't seem to gain her footing. He hadn't bumped into her that hard.

"Step back from me, the both of ye! My best slipper's gone astray and so has my earring. If either of ye step on them with yer clumsy boots, I'll have yer heads on a platter! I swear it!"

"I'm nay touching her," Magnus said as he backed up a step.

Sutherland agreed. As much as he hated leaving a lady in distress,